Johnny Castleseed

by Edward Ormondroyd

Illustrated by Diana Thewlis

Parnassus Press Oakland California • Houghton Mifflin Company Boston 1985

Library of Congress Cataloging in Publication Data

Ormondroyd, Edward.
    Johnny Castleseed.

    Summary: As Evan's father shows him how to make a
wonderful sandcastle, they see the idea spread and
grow in the minds of others on the beach, as if from
scattered seeds.
    1. Children's stories, American. [1. Sandcastles—
Fiction. 2. Seashore—Fiction] I. Thewlis, Diana, ill.
II. Title
PZ7.0635Jo   1985   [E]   85-8189
ISBN 0-395-38355-2

Printed in the United States of America

A PARNASSUS PRESS BOOK

H 10 9 8 7 6 5 4 3 2 1

One day Evan and his father walked to a beach in California. Their trail
went through the cool shadows of laurel trees and alders and buckeyes
and towering Douglas firs.

"Who planted all these trees?" Evan wanted to know.

"Nobody," his father said. "The seeds just fell from other trees. Maybe some of them were buried by squirrels or jays."

"I know who planted a whole lot of trees," Evan said. "We read about him in school."

"Oh? Who was that?"

"Johnny Appleseed. He walked all around the countryside in the old days, and everywhere he went he scattered apple seeds. And then apple trees grew up wherever he'd passed by."

"That was a terrific thing to do," Evan's father said. He thought for a
few minutes, and added, "Hey! How would you like to do something
like that?"

"Sure!"

"Well, I bet you can. Not *exactly* like that, maybe, but something like
it. Did you ever hear of Johnny Castleseed?"

"No. What did he do?"

"He walked all around the seacoasts and lakeshores, and everywhere there was sand he scattered castle seeds. And then castles grew up wherever he'd passed by. And it wasn't just in the old days, either. He's still doing it right now."

"Aw," Evan said. "Really?"

"Yup! I bet I can even show him to you when we get to the beach. I bet we can even help him plant some castles."

"Hmmm. What does he look like?"

"Oh, a little like you, and a little like me and something like everybody."

"Hmmm. What does a castle seed look like?"

"Well, it's a funny kind of seed—it doesn't really look like anything. But you know for sure that it's been planted when you see it growing."

"Aw," Evan said. "I don't believe there is such a thing. I don't believe there's any Johnny Castleseed, either. You're just making it up!"

But Evan's father only smiled a mysterious smile and said, "All right, all right. It's true—but let's see what happens."

After a long walk they finally came to the beach. "Race you to the water!" Evan shouted. They dashed across the sand, and Evan won. They

took off their shoes and socks, and waded in the icy water, picking up pebbles and shells that gleamed like jewels. On the tideline they found some kelp, and they both picked up a strand. Evan tried to crack his like a whip. Evan's father worked on his with his pocket knife, and made a horn that sounded like a trombone. Then they collected driftwood and built a fire, and sat down by it to eat their sandwiches.

When they were lazing around after lunch Evan said, "Darn! I wish I'd brought a bucket and shovel. I could've made a neat sand castle."

"You don't need any bucket and shovel," his father said. "You can make a beautiful castle with your bare hands. Come on, I'll show you."

There was a stream from the forest flowing across the beach. They stopped at a place beside it where the water was quiet, and began to build while Evan's father explained how:

All you need is very wet sand. If we didn't have this stream to get it from we could make a pool by digging down through the sand until we reached water level.

Now, plop a handful of wet sand down on the beach. See how it firms up and stays in a lump? That's because most of the water in it quickly drains down into the sand below. The water left in the lump acts like

glue, and makes the sand grains stick together. Don't try to plop your wet sand down on a rock or board—it won't hold its shape.

Take another wet handful and drop it on top of the first lump. See how it stays there? Like magic! You can go on piling one handful on another, and make a pillar.

If you drop your handfuls side by side, you can make a wall—a thick one or a thin one. The thicker it is, the higher you can go. If you drop your handfuls in a circle, around and around and up and up, you can make a hollow tower.

Towers and walls—it's beginning to look like a castle already! But you need to get in and out of a castle, so let's dig some archways through the walls. If you work carefully, and don't try to make them too wide, they won't collapse. You can make a nice smooth cut with a popsicle stick or a piece of shell. Let's cut some archways into the towers too. Can't you just see the little lords and ladies and soldiers walking in and out?

A canal? Sure—we can dig one right through this archway. Just work slowly and carefully so the water doesn't slosh around and make the arch crumble. That's it.

Look at all the things on the beach we can use to decorate our castle: sticks, seagull feathers, shells, pebbles—we could even pick flowers on the dunes over there. But watch: here's the fanciest decoration of all— more sand!

What you do is dribble it on. It's easy to learn the knack. Here, scoop some wet sand out of the stream. Turn the back of your hand up, and let the sand dribble down between your thumb and fingers. See how when a drop lands on the castle it flattens out into a little pat, like a mouse pancake? The next drop leaves another little pancake, either on top of the first, or next to it, or overlapping it. Of course, the water runs out between your thumb and fingers pretty fast. You have to scoop up more wet sand every few seconds. But look what you can do with it!

Let's fancy up the road you made leading up to that archway. Move your hand along the edge of the road while the sand dribbles out. Isn't that a neat little wall?

Or try this on top of one of the towers. Hold your hand still while the sand dribbles out. All the mouse pancakes stack up and up, and there— you've made a spire! Here, let's make a row of them all around the tops of the towers. Now we're getting some real style.

Here's the best trick of all—dribbled arches. Start with a spire. Make another spire about an inch away. Dribble a little on one spire, then a little on the other, back and forth, back and forth. Make them grow toward each other as they rise. Then the last magic drop falls right in the middle and connects them in an arch!

It takes practice. Don't get discouraged or mad if your spires fall down before you can connect them, or if the wind makes it hard to dribble the sand exactly where you want it. This happens to everybody. Just keep trying.

Now you've got it! Terrific! All right, you take that wall and I'll take this one. What we're going to do is make a row of connected arches all along the top. And then we'll dribble another row of smaller arches on top of the first. Our castle is going to be as beautiful as a Gothic cathedral…

While Evan and his father were building their castle, people stopped to watch them. Sometimes four or five people would be standing around and watching at the same time.

At last they were finished. It was a gorgeous castle! It had four towers

with thick walls between them, and archways and roads and ramps and a moat and a canal and spires and arches and seagull feather flags. Evan and his father stepped back to admire their work. Evan was so proud that he had to hug himself to keep from bursting.

But while they were looking, one of the dribbled arches collapsed.

"It's falling down!" Evan cried.

"I know," his father said. "It can't be helped, though. What holds it all together is water, and when the water begins to dry up, the sand grains start falling apart. So you can't keep a sand castle for very long. But that's all right—the real point is how much fun you had making it. And look! What did I tell you when we were walking through the trees? Look at that!"

He pointed up and down the beach. In one place, a boy and girl who had been watching them were beginning a castle of their own. In another place, a man and a woman who had been watching them were starting another castle.

"There you are, Evan! Johnny Castleseed just went by, scattering castle seeds. Didn't I tell you it was true?"

"You said you were going to show him to me," Evan said. "I didn't see him. I didn't see any castle seeds, either."

"No, you can't see a castle seed—it's an idea, not a thing. Somebody builds a sand castle. Somebody else comes along, and watches, and thinks, 'Hey, that looks like fun—I'm going to try it, too!' And right then and there a castle seed is planted."

"But where was Johnny Castleseed?"

"Right here, Evan! Those people were watching *us* when the castle seeds were planted, weren't they? So Johnny Castleseed is—?"

"Oh!" Evan shouted. "ME!"

"Right!"

"And YOU!"

"Right! And anybody else who does what we did."

So the two Johnny Castleseeds went over and watched the man and woman build their castle, and then they watched the boy and girl build their castle. And they noticed that some of the other watchers had a gleam in their eyes that said, 'Hmmm, that looks like fun. I'm going to try it, too'—the gleam of a newly-planted castle seed.

And then, with the sun behind them, they started the long walk back through the cool, darkening forest.